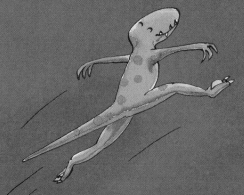

Dinosaurumpus!

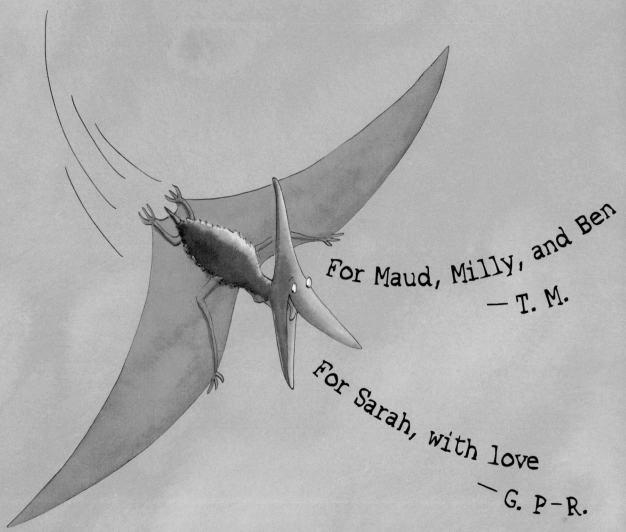

For Maud, Milly, and Ben
— T. M.

For Sarah, with love
— G. P-R.

This book was originally published in Great Britain in 2002 by Orchard Books London, and in the United States in 2003 by Orchard Books.

ISBN-13: 978-0-439-39516-8
ISBN-10: 0-439-39516-X

12 11 10 9 8 7 6 5   12 13 14/0

Printed in the U.S.A.
First Bookshelf edition, March 2009

Dinosaurumpus!

By Tony Mitton

Illustrated by Guy Parker-Rees

SCHOLASTIC INC.
New York   Toronto   London   Auckland   Sydney
Mexico City   New Delhi   Hong Kong   Buenos Aires

There's a quake and a quiver
and a rumbling around.

It makes you shiver.
It's a thundery sound.

"Shake, shake, shudder...
near the sludgy old swamp.
The dinosaurs are coming.
Get ready to romp.

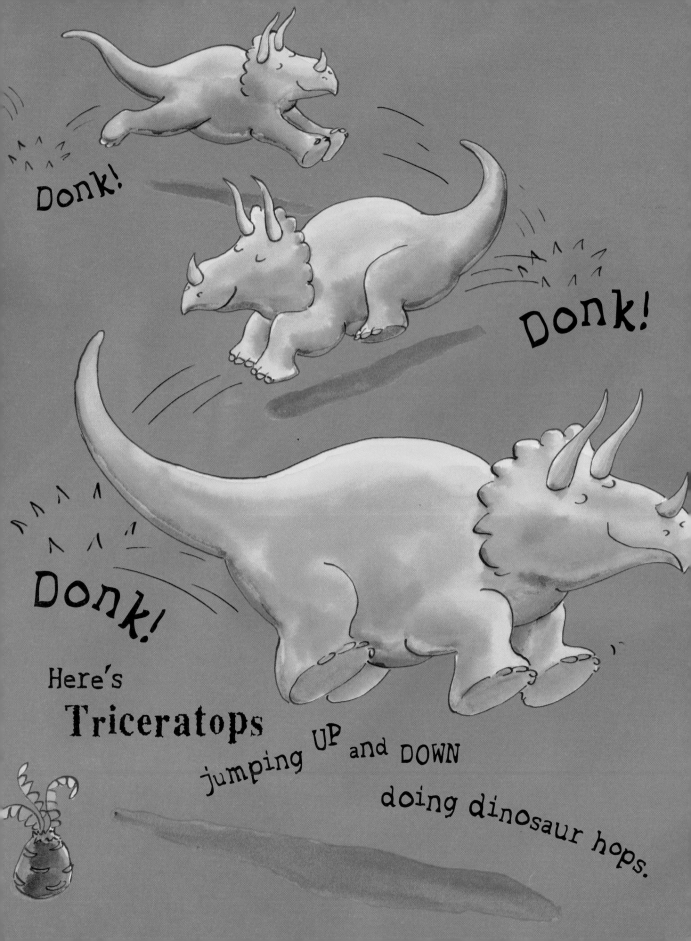

Donk!

Donk!

Donk!

Here's **Triceratops** jumping UP and DOWN doing dinosaur hops.

He wears three horns on his **big**, bony head,

and thunders along with a **Bomp! Bomp!** tread.

"Shake, shake, shudder"... near the sludgy old swamp. The dinosaurs are coming. Get ready to romp.

Watch out for **Deinosuchus** with her **snip-snap** grin, as she perches on her tail and **twists** in a spin.

Stegosaurus stomps along
with lots of her playmates.

Clatter! Clatter! Clatter!

go their bony
back plates.

"Shake, shake, shudder"...
near the sludgy old swamp.
The dinosaurs are coming.
Get ready to romp.

Styracosaurus shakes his collar and his spikes. Rattle! Rattle! Rattle! is the noise that he likes!

Clatter!

Rattle!

Zoom! Zoom!

Come and take a peek...

"Shake, shake, shudder...
near the sludgy old swamp.
Everybody's doing the
dinosaur romp.

ROOAA

ROAR! ROAR! ROAR!
What's making that sound?
The dinosaurs stop
and there's silence around.

rrrr...!

Roar! Roar! Roar!
Now we're shivering with fright.
What can make a noise like that
in the night?

He's huge
and he's heavy,
but all he wants to do...

The dinosaurs won't scratch us, or bite us, or thump us. They just want to holler up a...

rumpus!

"Shake, shake, shudder...
near the sludgy old swamp.
Everybody's doing the
dinosaur romp.

But soon all the rompers grow sleepy and slow.

The rumpus calms down and the sound drops low.

The rompers drift together
and tumble in a heap...

'til finally the dinosaurs
        are all fast asleep.

And now the only noise
in the deep of the night
is...

dinosaur-snoring 'til the next day's light.